CIVIC PARTICIPATION
Working for Civil Rights

LGBTQ HUMAN RIGHTS MOVEMENT

Theresa Morlock

New York

Published in 2017 by The Rosen Publishing Group, Inc.
29 East 21st Street, New York, NY 10010

Copyright © 2017 by The Rosen Publishing Group, Inc.

All rights reserved. No part of this book may be reproduced in any form without permission in writing from the publisher, except by a reviewer.

First Edition

Editor: Caitie McAneney
Book Design: Mickey Harmon

Photo Credits: Cover (image) Davies, Diana/The New York Public Library Digital Collections, pp. 1, 3–32 (background) Milena_Bo/Shutterstock.com; p. 5 Lindsay Douglas/Shutterstock.com; p. 7 Michael Stewart/Contributor/Getty Images Entertainment/Getty Images; p. 9 Bikeworldtravel/Shutterstock.com; p. 10 New York Daily News Archive/Contributor/New York Daily News/Getty Images; p. 11 New York Post Archives/Contributors/The New York Post/Getty Images; p. 13 Bettmann/Contributor/Bettmann/Getty Images; p. 15 (main) Miami Herald/Contributor/Tribune News Service/Getty Images; p. 15 (inset) Steve Liss/Contributor/The LIFE Images Collection/Getty Images; p. 17 CREATISTA/Shutterstock.com; p. 19 The Washington Post/Contributor/The Washington Post/Getty Images; p. 21 Rawpixel.com/Shutterstock.com; p. 23 Raleigh News & Observer/Contributor/Tribune News Service/Getty Images; p. 25 (main) Tom Williams/Contributor/CQ-Roll Call Group/Getty Images; p. 25 (Harvey Milk) Bettmann/Contributor/Bettmann/Getty Images; p. 27 rmnoa357/Shutterstock.com; p. 29 Sergey Novikov/Shutterstock.com.

Cataloging-in-Publication Data
Names: Morlock, Theresa.
Title: LGBTQ human rights movement / Theresa Morlock.
Description: New York : PowerKids Press, 2017. | Series: Civic participation: working for civil rights | Includes index.
Identifiers: ISBN 9781499426816 (pbk.) | ISBN 9781499428513 (library bound) | ISBN 9781499426823 (6 pack)
Subjects: LCSH: Gay rights–Juvenile literature. | Homosexuality–Juvenile literature.
Classification: LCC HQ76.26 M8417 2017 | DDC 306.76'60835-dc23

Manufactured in the United States of America

CONTENTS

What's LGBTQ? 4
Gender Identity 6
Homophobia and Transphobia 8
The Stonewall Riots 10
The AIDS Crisis 12
Hate Crimes 14
Marriage for All 16
Don't Ask, Don't Tell 18
Employment Discrimination 20
Current Issues 22
Advocacy 24
Be an Ally 26
Looking Forward 28
Glossary 31
Index 32
Websites 32

WHAT'S LGBTQ?

LGBTQ stands for lesbian, gay, bisexual, transgender, and queer or questioning. These words are used to describe a person's **sexual orientation** or their **gender** identity. Gender identity is the gender a person identifies as, regardless of **anatomy** they were born with.

Women who identify as lesbian are attracted to other women, while men who identify as gay are attracted to other men. Bisexual people are attracted to both men and women. A transgender person is someone whose gender identity is different from the anatomy they were born with. The term "queer" can refer to the whole LGBT community or to those who identify with other labels that fall outside of LGBT. Some individuals question their sexuality and gender identity because they don't identify with what is considered "normal." The LGBTQ movement has made great strides in creating a future where all people can live their true identities.

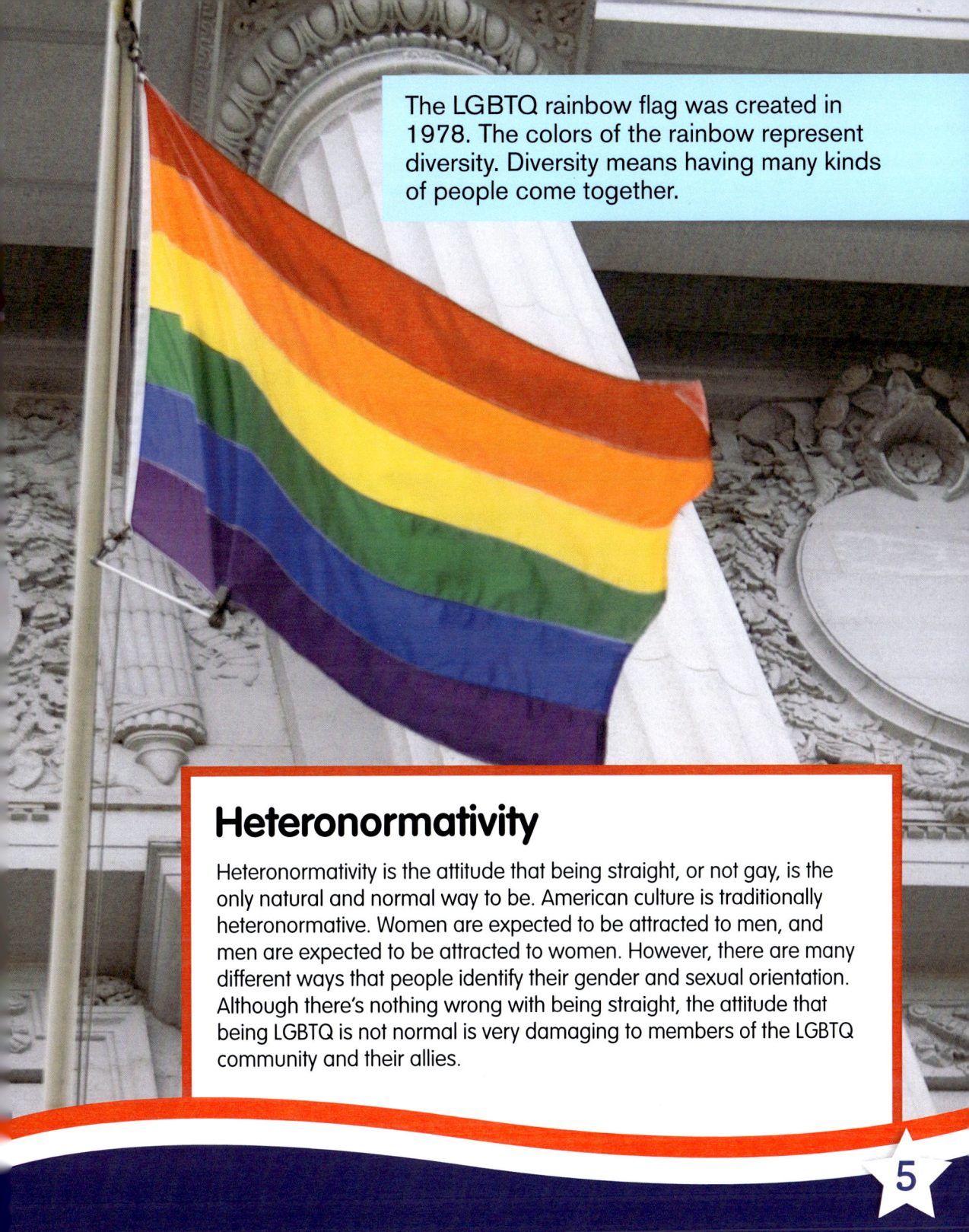

The LGBTQ rainbow flag was created in 1978. The colors of the rainbow represent diversity. Diversity means having many kinds of people come together.

Heteronormativity

Heteronormativity is the attitude that being straight, or not gay, is the only natural and normal way to be. American culture is traditionally heteronormative. Women are expected to be attracted to men, and men are expected to be attracted to women. However, there are many different ways that people identify their gender and sexual orientation. Although there's nothing wrong with being straight, the attitude that being LGBTQ is not normal is very damaging to members of the LGBTQ community and their allies.

GENDER IDENTITY

As soon as a person is born, they're labeled as male or female based on their anatomy. Gender is the way people are expected to act based on the anatomy they're born with. Many of our ideas about gender are based on **stereotypes**. For example, one stereotype is that boys shouldn't cry. Another is that girls can't be strong.

However, in recent years, people have begun to recognize that gender is more **complicated** than that. There aren't just two options—male and female—that are based on anatomy. Many people who were born male identify as female, and many people who were born female identify as male. In the past, many transgender people kept their inner identities a secret. However, quite recently, people have started coming forward to raise awareness about what being transgender means.

Jazz Jennings was the grand marshal of the 2016 Pride Parade in New York City. This transgender teen is changing the world by sharing her story!

Jazz Jennings

Jazz Jennings is a transgender teen **activist** for LGBTQ issues. Jazz was born with male anatomy, but has identified as a girl since she was a toddler. Her story, which she shared in the film *I Am Jazz: A Family in Transition*, showed people that children and teens can be transgender. Jazz speaks at medical schools, conferences, and colleges to raise awareness about transgender youth. She started a company, Purple Rainbow Tails, to raise money for the cause and is the honorary cofounder of the Transkids Purple Rainbow Foundation.

HOMOPHOBIA AND TRANSPHOBIA

Homophobia and transphobia are the fear of, or **prejudice** against, gay and lesbian or transgender people. For many years, gay, lesbian, and transgender individuals were treated as if they were sick or **immoral**. Being gay was thought of as a mental illness or a crime that could be legally punished. This attitude made it difficult and unsafe for LGBTQ people to live openly.

Homophobia and transphobia often lead to bullying—both physical and emotional—against LGBTQ people. LGBTQ youth are at a higher risk of **harassment**, violence, bullying, and teasing than straight and cisgender, or non-transgender, youth. As such, they are also more likely to deal with **depression**, attempt to take their own life, and use drugs. The prejudice against LGBTQ individuals extends past the school years, though. LGBTQ adults face higher rates of harassment and **discrimination** at work.

Many people who identify as gay or transgender continue to face bullying and intolerance today.

THE STONEWALL RIOTS

During the 1960s, Greenwich Village in New York City was a popular home for many LGBTQ individuals. At this time, many laws targeted LGBTQ people. A branch of the police force called the Public Morals Squad harassed LGBTQ people. In 1969, the Public Morals Squad entered a gay nightclub called the Stonewall Inn and made many arrests. These arrests were common, but this time, community members fought back, protesting the treatment of gay and lesbian people. The first gay pride march was part of these protests.

riot outside Stonewall Inn

The Stonewall riots drew the country's attention to the problem of discrimination against LGBTQ individuals.

The Stonewall riots are now thought of as the start of the modern LGBTQ movement. LGBTQ activist groups such as the Gay Liberation Front and the Gay Activists Alliance were formed. These groups raised awareness about LGBTQ people and stood up to discrimination against them.

THE AIDS CRISIS

During the 1980s, issues of LGBTQ discrimination were brought into the spotlight with the AIDS **crisis**. AIDS is a deadly disease that lessens the body's ability to fight illness. In the 1980s, most of the people affected by AIDS were gay men. Although AIDS can affect anyone, it was wrongly blamed on gay people, who were thought of as immoral.

Many people with AIDS at this time faced cruelty and the loss of homes and jobs. Some were refused medical care. They often died painful deaths. The LGBTQ community came together to help people suffering from AIDS. On October 11, 1987, thousands of activists marched to the White House in Washington, D.C., to demand action and raise awareness about AIDS and LGBTQ discrimination.

Many activists that worked for equal rights for people suffering from AIDS had the illness themselves. Pictured here are members of the AIDS protest group ACT UP demonstrating in front of the White House on June 1, 1987. They are demanding more money for AIDS research.

Ryan White CARE Act

In 1984, a 13-year-old boy named Ryan White was diagnosed with AIDS. When officials at Ryan's school learned about his illness, they told him he couldn't go there anymore. In 1987, Ryan began to speak publicly about his experience with AIDS and the discrimination he suffered because of it. His efforts to educate the public about the disease helped win AIDS patients more support. In 1990, the Ryan White CARE Act was passed to give better care to AIDS patients.

HATE CRIMES

A hate crime is an act of violence based on prejudice. Throughout U.S. history, people have been beaten and even murdered for identifying as LGBTQ. One of the key events in the LGBTQ movement was the signing of the Matthew Shepard and James Byrd Jr. Hate Crimes Prevention Act on October 28, 2009. Before this act, the federal government only considered hate crimes to be those based on race, religion, or nationality, not sexual orientation, gender identity, or disability. The act was an important step in legally protecting LGBTQ people.

Unfortunately, hate crimes against LGBTQ people continue to take place. In June 2016, 49 people were murdered at a nightclub in Orlando, Florida, that was regularly visited by members of the LGBTQ community. It was the deadliest mass shooting in the United States to date.

After the Orlando shooting, many people came together to speak out against violence and declare that love will win over hate.

Matthew Shepard

Matthew Shepard was a student at the University of Wyoming. He loved to travel and learn about the different people of the world. In 1998, when Matthew was just 21, he was attacked by two men who targeted him because he was gay. He was beaten so badly that he died a few days later. Matthew's parents created a foundation in his honor, and they've spent years spreading his message of acceptance and love.

MARRIAGE FOR ALL

One of the key issues in the fight for LGBTQ equality is marriage for same-sex couples. Those who argue against marriage for same-sex couples often base their arguments on religious beliefs and traditional ideas of marriage. Signed in 1996, the Defense of Marriage Act kept same-sex couples from receiving federal marriage benefits and allowed states to refuse to recognize marriages between same-sex couples.

In effect, the Defense of Marriage Act legalized discrimination against LGBTQ couples. However, individual states began to make marriages between same-sex couples legal on the state level. After years of the LGBTQ community and its supporters fighting for equal marriage rights, marriage for same-sex couples became legal in all 50 states on June 26, 2015. Unfortunately, some states still make it difficult for same-sex couples to marry.

The message of the LGBTQ movement is "Love is love." Legal marriage equality is an important step in the country's acceptance of the LGBTQ community and all marriages and families.

DON'T ASK, DON'T TELL

For many years, military codes punished soldiers who were suspected of being gay. A policy in 1982 officially banned all gay men and lesbians from the military. Thousands of LGBTQ individuals were discharged, or fired, from their positions. The Don't Ask, Don't Tell policy went into effect in 1993. It stated that gay or lesbian people could enlist in the military, but they must keep their sexual orientation a secret.

LGBTQ service members had to live with the fear of being found out because of this policy. In 2010, the U.S. Senate voted to repeal the Don't Ask, Don't Tell policy. For the first time in history, gay men and lesbians became free to enlist in the military and serve openly. As of June 30, 2016, transgender people are permitted the same freedoms.

Pictured here are veterans protesting the Don't Ask, Don't Tell policy. These men are part of the Gay, Lesbian, Bisexual Veterans of America, which is now known as the American Veterans for Equal Rights.

Stephen Snyder-Hill

Stephen Snyder-Hill served in the military during the Gulf War and in Iraq. His service earned him many medals and honors. In 2011, Snyder-Hill asked members of the Republican party if they would undo the repeal of the Don't Ask, Don't Tell policy during a debate. This question caused people to become upset. The audience booed his video, which shed a national spotlight on his concerns. Stephen continues to speak out about discrimination in the military.

EMPLOYMENT DISCRIMINATION

In the past, the government allowed discrimination in places of employment. Anyone suspected of being gay could be fired. In 1953, President Dwight D. Eisenhower signed Executive Order 10450, which labeled any person who wasn't straight as immoral. Thousands of workers lost their government jobs as a result of this order. Its broader effect was that it made discrimination against LGBTQ people legal and publicly acceptable.

In 2013, the Employment Non-Discrimination Act was proposed to protect all workers from discrimination based on gender identity or sexual orientation. The act sought to protect workers from being harassed, denied work benefits, or kept from job opportunities based on gender identity, **gender transition**, or sexual orientation. Unfortunately, the act never passed.

Laws and policies are necessary to protect the rights of LGBTQ people in the workplace.

CURRENT ISSUES

An issue that highlights LGBTQ discrimination is House Bill 2, which was passed on March 23, 2016, in North Carolina. The bill requires that all people in the state use bathrooms and locker rooms that match the anatomy they were born with. This means that a transgender person who was born with female anatomy but identifies as male would be forced to use a bathroom for females. House Bill 2 has caused a huge public reaction because LGBTQ supporters worry that it means a step backward in the movement for equal rights.

Legislation like House Bill 2 highlights how LGBTQ people continue to face prejudice in public places. Many people still hold the belief that anyone who is not straight is a threat. In spite of victories in the LGBTQ movement, many still suffer from harassment and intolerance.

House Bill 2 discriminates against transgender people because it denies their gender identity and labels them male or female based on the anatomy they were born with. This picture shows a rally in support of House Bill 2 behind the North Carolina General Assembly building in Raleigh, North Carolina, on April 25, 2016.

ADVOCACY

Advocacy means supporting and working for a cause. The largest LGBTQ rights group in the country is the Human Rights Campaign (HRC). Organizations such as the HRC and the American Civil Liberties Union work to make sure that all people are given basic human rights and can live in a safe environment.

A big part of advocacy is educating the public. Civil rights groups encourage people to know what their rights are and how to defend them. They also raise awareness about issues of prejudice and intolerance. The more people know about discrimination against LGBTQ people, the harder they may fight to end it. Advocates also speak to politicians to push for policy changes. The most important step in ending discrimination is teaching acceptance and understanding.

July 12, 2016, marked the one-month anniversary of the Orlando shooting. Here, the president of the HRC, Chad Griffin, speaks during a vigil in Washington, D.C., with pictures of the victims held up behind him.

Harvey Milk

Harvey Milk was one of the first openly gay U.S. officials. He was elected to office in San Francisco in 1977, a time when homophobia was widespread. After serving in the Navy after college, he became involved with the LGBTQ community in Greenwich Village and later in San Francisco, where he became an activist. Only a year after he was elected, Milk was killed by a politician who disagreed with his policies.

BE AN ALLY

An ally is someone who stands up for people. You can be an ally to the LGBTQ community no matter what your gender or sexual orientation is. Allies support LGBTQ individuals and speak out against injustice.

You can show your support for equality by participating in **demonstrations** supporting LGBTQ pride. Every year, schools across the country take part in a Day of Silence, which is led by the Gay, Lesbian, and Straight Education Network. On this day, students promise not to speak in an effort to show the effects of bullying on LGBTQ students. Every June, the country celebrates LGBT Pride month to celebrate diversity and honor the impact LGBTQ people have had on history. Many cities host parades so that everyone can show their support for the LGTBQ community and allies.

The best way to be an ally is to be a friend. Be open to learning about other people, even if they're different from you.

LOOKING FORWARD

Many of the victories of the LGBTQ movement have taken place only in the past few years. There are still many more challenges to overcome.

The greatest danger to the LGBTQ movement is the attitude of suspicion and prejudice with which LGBTQ individuals have been treated throughout history. Changing the way we look at gender and sexual orientation will help protect LGBTQ people so they are no longer abused or judged unfairly.

Love and acceptance are the foundations of the LGBTQ movement. The message of the movement is that all people are worthy of respect, no matter their race, nationality, gender, or sexual orientation. Together, we can help build a future where all people can be themselves, free from fear and discrimination.

Whether you identify as LGBTQ or straight, transgender or cisgender, you can be a supporter of this important human rights movement.

TIMELINE OF THE LGBTQ RIGHTS MOVEMENT

1978
The rainbow flag is created as a symbol of support for the LGBTQ community.

January 28, 1982
A policy officially bans gay men from serving in the U.S. military.

October 11, 1987
Thousands of people march in Washington, D.C., to raise awareness of AIDS and to protest discrimination.

October 1, 1993
The Don't Ask, Don't Tell policy is passed.

April 25, 1993
An estimated 1 million people attend the March on Washington for Lesbian, Gay and Bi Equal Rights and Liberation.

September 21, 1996
President Bill Clinton signs the Defense of Marriage Act.

December 18, 2010
The U.S. Senate votes to repeal the Don't Ask, Don't Tell policy.

June 26, 2015
Same-sex marriage becomes legal in all 50 states.

June 12, 2016
Pulse nightclub is attacked in Orlando, Florida, and 49 people are killed.

June 30, 2016
The ban on transgender people serving in the military is lifted.

GLOSSARY

activist: Someone who acts strongly in support of or against an issue.

anatomy: A person's body.

complicated: Having many parts; difficult to understand.

crisis: A difficult or serious situation that needs attention.

demonstration: An event in which people gather to show that they support or oppose something.

depression: A sickness in which a person feels sad and hopeless and often lacks energy.

discrimination: Treating people unequally because of their race, beliefs, background, or lifestyle.

gender: The behavioral or mental traits typically associated with one sex.

gender transition: A time when a person begins living as the gender with which they identify rather that the one they were labeled at birth.

harassment: To make repeated attacks against someone, either verbally or physically.

immoral: Against generally held principles of behavior or morals.

prejudice: An unfair feeling of dislike for someone because of race, religion, gender identity, or sexual orientation.

sexual orientation: A person's attraction to members of the same and/or opposite sex.

stereotype: The act of unfairly believing that all people with a certain characteristic are the same.

INDEX

A
AIDS, 12, 13, 30
American Civil Liberties Union, 24

D
Day of Silence, 26
Defense of Marriage Act, 16, 30
Don't Ask, Don't Tell, 18, 19, 30

E
Eisenhower, Dwight D., 20
Employment Non-Discrimination Act, 20
Executive Order 10450, 20

G
Gay Activists Alliance, 11
Gay, Lesbian, and Straight Education Network, 26
Gay Liberation Front, 11
Greenwich Village, 10, 25

H
hate crime, 14, 15
House Bill 2, 22, 23
Human Rights Campaign, 24, 25

J
Jennings, Jazz, 7

M
marriage equality, 16, 17, 30
Matthew Shepard and James Byrd Jr. Hate Crimes Prevention Act, 14
Milk, Harvey, 25

N
New York City, 7, 10
North Carolina, 22, 23

O
Orlando, 14, 15, 25, 30

P
Pride March, 7
Public Morals Squad, 10

R
Ryan White CARE Act, 13

S
San Francisco, 25
Shepard, Matthew, 15
Snyder-Hill, Stephen, 19
Stonewall riots, 10, 11

W
Washington, D.C., 12, 19, 25, 30
White, Ryan, 13

WEBSITES

Due to the changing nature of Internet links, PowerKids Press has developed an online list of websites related to the subject of this book. This site is updated regularly. Please use this link to access the list: www.powerkidslinks.com/civic/lgbtq